GANDERS

Ethel
the Chicken

written and illustrated by
COLIN THOMPSON

HODDER AND STOUGHTON
London   Sydney   Auckland   Toronto

British Library Cataloguing in Publication Data

Thompson, Colin
  Ethel the chicken.
  I. Title   II. Series
  823.914

  ISBN 0-340-53107-X

Text and illustrations copyright © Colin Thompson 1991

First published 1991

Published by Hodder and Stoughton Children's Books,
a division of Hodder and Stoughton Ltd,
Mill Road, Dunton Green, Sevenoaks, Kent TN13 2YA

Photoset by En to En, Tunbridge Wells, Kent

Printed in Great Britain by T. J. Press (Padstow) Ltd,
Padstow, Cornwall

1 Neville

At the end of a quiet street at the edge of the town stood an old empty house. Behind the house, at the bottom of the overgrown garden, in a wooden box hidden under a bramble bush, lived a chicken called Ethel. On the side of the box was a label that said FIRST CLASS ORANGES. Even though chickens are nearly as stupid as sheep, Ethel knew that she was not an orange.

'I am a chicken,' she said.

'Prove it,' said a young rat called Neville, who lived in a paper-bag nest under the old house. He was only a child and had never seen an orange or a chicken before.

'Wow, a talking chicken!' shouted an ant, but no one could hear her because she was very, very small, and before she could rush off and tell her four hundred and eighty brothers and sisters Ethel ate her.

'Listen, rat,' said Ethel, 'oranges are round and don't have feathers and don't lay eggs.'

'They might,' said Neville.

'You're a stupid little rat,' said Ethel. 'Nearly as stupid as a sheep.' And she laid an egg.

'Is that an orange?' asked Neville.

'Of course not, it's an egg,' snapped Ethel.

'But it's round and got no feathers,' said Neville.

Before Ethel could say anything else,
Neville's mother came rushing down the
lawn and grabbed him by the ear.

'How many times have I told you not to
talk to strange fruit?' she said as she
dragged him off.

Ethel settled back down on her nest and
looked through the tall grass at the old
house. It was a very long time since
anyone had come out into the garden.

It's probably an hour, she thought to herself. The old lady who had lived in the house had gone away ages ago but chickens can't tell the time. She knew she hadn't been given any corn that morning but she'd had an enormous worm and a couple of lovely slugs for breakfast so she wasn't hungry.

When the old lady's children had come and taken all the furniture away they hadn't seen Ethel. They had come out into the back garden and folded up the deckchairs, but Ethel had heard them talking about chicken and chips and had sat very still under the rhubarb until they'd gone. They'd closed the curtains, locked the doors and driven off in a red car.

Ethel felt that there was more to life than eating worms and slugs and laying eggs, but she didn't know what it was. She tried to think about it but chickens' brains aren't very good at thinking and every time she tried to she fell asleep. As she sat there dozing away in the afternoon sunshine, young Neville came back.

'My mum says I've got to come and say sorry for being cheeky to you,' he said. Ethel said it was all right and that she was sure he was quite a good boy really. 'Can I be your friend?' asked Neville.

'Of course you can,' said the old hen, and they chatted about this and that for a while. Neville said his mum had been in a bad mood ever since the old lady had gone.

'We used to eat cake and toffees,'
he explained, 'but now the house is empty
we have to eat woodlice all the time.'

'I like woodlice,' said Ethel. But then,
she had never eaten cake.

'I don't,' said Neville. 'All the bits stick in
your teeth.'

'I haven't got teeth,' Ethel told him. 'I like
the way their legs tickle as you swallow
them.'

Neville looked a bit green at this and
said he had to go and help his dad chew
up some paper-bags. Ethel told him to
come and see her any time he felt like it.
When he had gone she realised what the
other thing was that she had been trying to
think of. It was loneliness.

2 Loneliness

Since the old lady had gone, no one had come to see her. Every morning the old lady had come down the garden with a mug of corn and every morning she had tickled the top of Ethel's head and talked to her. Most of the time Ethel hadn't been able to understand what the old lady had been talking about but the words had always felt warm and comforting in her ears. Ethel was old herself and hardly ever laid an egg but the old lady had never seemed to mind.

It was only now, since the young rat had started visiting her, that she realised how much she missed the old lady and how lonely she was. The hedgehogs who came and took the occasional egg she rolled out of her box were a miserable lot. You couldn't talk to them at all. When Ethel tried they just grunted a bit and shuffled off into the undergrowth. The other birds laughed at her because she was big and lumpy and couldn't fly and next-door's cat just sneered at her. But then next-door's cat sneered at everybody.

The next day young Neville came to see
Ethel again. He told her about all sorts of
wonderful things she had never heard of
like skateboards and calculators. But when
Ethel tried to talk about slugs, Neville
grew restless and sat there fidgeting and
sucking bits of woodlouse out of his teeth.
Eventually he wandered off saying he had
to help his dad again.

It was a lovely hot summer afternoon. Ethel sank into her nest, half asleep, and clucked softly to herself. Bright butterflies skipped in and out of the dandelion flowers, whistling the latest tune. Ethel had never eaten a butterfly and wondered what they tasted like. She didn't know that they were just caterpillars with their best clothes on.

She could hear children playing in the
garden next door. She liked children.
The old lady had brought some to see her
once and they'd all tickled her feathers
and cuddled her. It had made her feel
very happy.

She thought about going next door to
see the children but there was a big
hedge and a tall fence all round the
garden, far too tall for a fat old chicken to
get over. At her age, it was all she could
do to jump up on to the roof of her box.
A diet of juicy worms and slugs had made
her so fat that sometimes, as she waddled
round the lawn, she tripped over her own
feet. It was no fun being old and even
worse being lonely and old.

'You ought to try and get out a bit more,' said Neville's mum, when Ethel said she felt lonely. 'There's all sorts of things going on round the garden.'

'I'm too old for all that,' said Ethel. 'All I want is my old lady to come back.'

'You should go and meet the rabbits down by the apple trees,' Neville's mum went on, but there was no cheering Ethel up.

'I just want it to be like it used to be,' she said sadly.

3 Winter

The summer drifted lazily on. Neville came
to see Ethel less and less. He wanted to
play with his friends, to chase squirrels
and tease next-door's cat, not listen to an
old chicken talk about slugs. Neville's
mother didn't come any more either, not
now she had seven new children to look
after. Ethel couldn't blame them, she knew
she was boring. Sometimes just the simple
effort of looking for worms seemed too
much. In the good old days there had
always been a magic in scratching away
at the earth and jumping back, head to
one side, to find some new treasure.
Now everything seemed to have lost its

taste. Grass, worms, daffodils or slugs,
it was all the same. Only woodlice had any
sweetness left and they seemed to run
faster than they used to and be harder to
catch.

The first leaves began to fall and a breath of cold crept into the garden. The children next door stopped playing outside and the air was filled with the thick smoke of autumn as everybody piled up the dying plants into smouldering bonfires. In Ethel's garden the dead flowers shrivelled up with no one to clear them away. They hung over like thin skeletons and in the mornings were stiff with frost. The golden leaves turned brown and collected in damp piles on the lawn.

The days grew dark and short as winter covered the world. Ethel hid deep in her straw and tried to sleep. The slugs had finished and the worms had gone deeper into the earth. A few spiders still survived the cold and it was those that kept her going.

Rain came and broke up the old flowers and washed them into the ground. It washed the label off Ethel's box and dripped in through the cracks in the wood. It ran down her face so that if you had seen her you would have said you'd seen a chicken cry. The dampness crept into her bones and made them creak and her loneliness seemed to grow as dark as the winter nights.

She cheered up a bit when the snow
came. It made the garden bright and
clean. It covered her box with a thick coat
that kept her warm and dry and it lasted
for weeks. Neville began to visit her again
and although Ethel knew he was only
coming to get away from his baby brothers
and sisters, she was glad to see him.
He made a tunnel under the snow right
across the lawn and sat shivering in front
of Ethel's box, telling her all his news.

'My dad's been eaten by next-door's cat,'
he said, through chattering teeth. 'And my
brother Trevor.'

Ethel couldn't think of anything to say so
she tucked the young rat up in the straw
next to her and clucked. It started to snow
again, great big flakes that seemed to float
around for ages before they landed.

'Why's it so cold?' said Neville, who had
never seen a winter before.

'I don't know,' said Ethel. 'It always
seems to be cold when it snows.'

'Is it going to be like this for ever?'
he asked.

'Oh no, it always goes away again,' said
Ethel.

'What, back up in the sky?'

'I don't think so.'

'Well, where does it go?' asked Neville.

'I don't know,' she replied.

Neville's little sister, Tracy, popped up
out of the tunnel and jumped up and down
in front of them, blowing out white puffs of
cold breath.

'Mum says you've got to come home,' she squeaked. 'We've run out of paper-bags.'

Neville climbed out of the warm and followed his little sister back down the tunnel. Ethel closed her eyes and dreamt of the old lady surrounded by sunshine and fresh grass.

4 Comings and Goings

The snow melted, more rain came and went, and then one day the air seemed to be a little warmer. The sun grew bigger and stayed in the sky longer each day and opened new buds on the sleeping trees. Ethel got up and scratched about on the lawn. She found herself wandering further and further from her box into corners of the garden she had long forgotten.

The rheumatism in her bones seemed to fade until she could no longer hear her joints creaking. She fluttered right up into an old apple tree and sat there feeling quite pleased with herself.

As she sat there fluffing her feathers out, one of the curtains at the back of the house opened and a man looked out. She kept very still. One by one all the curtains were opened, windows and doors too. Ethel kept so still that her legs went to sleep and she fell out of the tree. She lay in the grass but no one came. No one had seen her and after a while the man shut the doors and windows and went away.

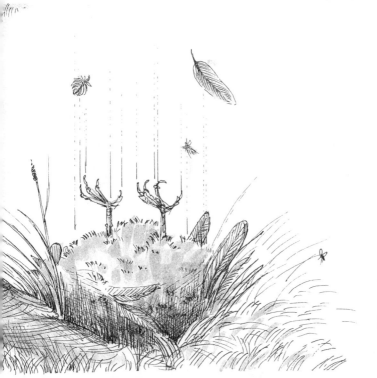

Later on Neville slipped out of the
shadows and jumped into Ethel's box.

'I'm not happy,' he said, sounding quite
grown up. 'Humans and rats are not
friends.'

'Don't be silly,' said Ethel. 'The old lady
was wonderful.'

'She was old,' said Neville. 'She didn't
know we were there. Most people don't
like us and try and kill us.'

'What on earth for?' asked Ethel.

'My mum says it's because we chew
their slippers,' said Neville.

Ethel didn't know what slippers were and when Neville told her she got that horrid taste in her mouth you get when someone sucks a handkerchief. She said she was sure he was wrong and anyway, perhaps the old lady was coming back. But she didn't. Over the next few weeks the man brought lots of people to the house but none of them was the old lady. Ethel sat quietly in her box and no one saw her. She knew in her heart that the young rat was probably right and she grew nervous at all the coming and going.

A few days later Neville and his mother came to say goodbye.

'We're going to live in this wonderful drain with my cousin Kevin,' said Neville, all excited. 'It goes right under the best restaurant in town. The rubbish is really great.'

Ethel felt very sad when they had gone. She even ignored a giant slug that slithered right in front of her box.

5 New Friends

One day some people came to the house and stayed. They took down all the old grey curtains and put up new ones covered in big red flowers. At night the windows were filled with yellow light that poured out on to the lawn. New smells drifted down the garden, wonderful warm smells that Ethel had never experienced before. There was still no sign of the old lady. A man came out on Saturday and cut the grass. He passed right by Ethel hiding in the back of her box, but he never saw her.

Then, as if by magic, there were children in the garden. A boy and a girl running and laughing, climbing the trees and swinging from the branches. Round and round they ran, throwing a big blue ball in the air. A big blue ball which bounced and rolled and rolled and rolled right up to Ethel's box.

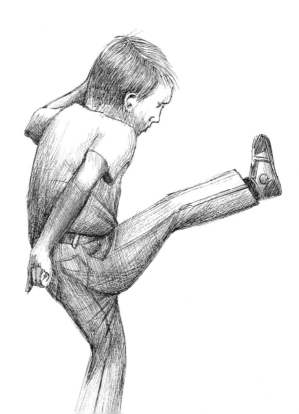

'Look, look, look,' shouted the little girl to her brother. They reached out and tickled Ethel in exactly the right place. She shut her eyes and felt all her loneliness slip away.

The little girl tucked Ethel under her arm and carried her up to the house. The little boy ran beside her, smiling and laughing.

Later on, the man gave Ethel a smart new box with a label on the side that said BEST APPLES. 'I am a chicken,' said Ethel to herself as she settled down into her wonderful new straw.

'And I shall call you Doris,' said the little girl as she poured her out a mug of corn.